In his debut as an author, my friend Jason Biggs
wrote this amazing book titled, "My Daddy Cuts My Hair."
This book is based off of real life experience,
describing what it's like to be a young boy
getting their first haircut.
For so many young boys,
getting their first haircut is a big deal,
it's even more special
when their dad is the one creating this first memory.

Congratulations on publishing your first book, Jason.
I wish you many blessings and much continued success.

Dontay Stevenson

Dedicated to
my son Eli Jaylin Biggs.

This is
my Daddy!

And
this is
my hair!

Sometimes,
I watch my daddy
shave and cut his hair.

The sound
of the machines
sounds scary!

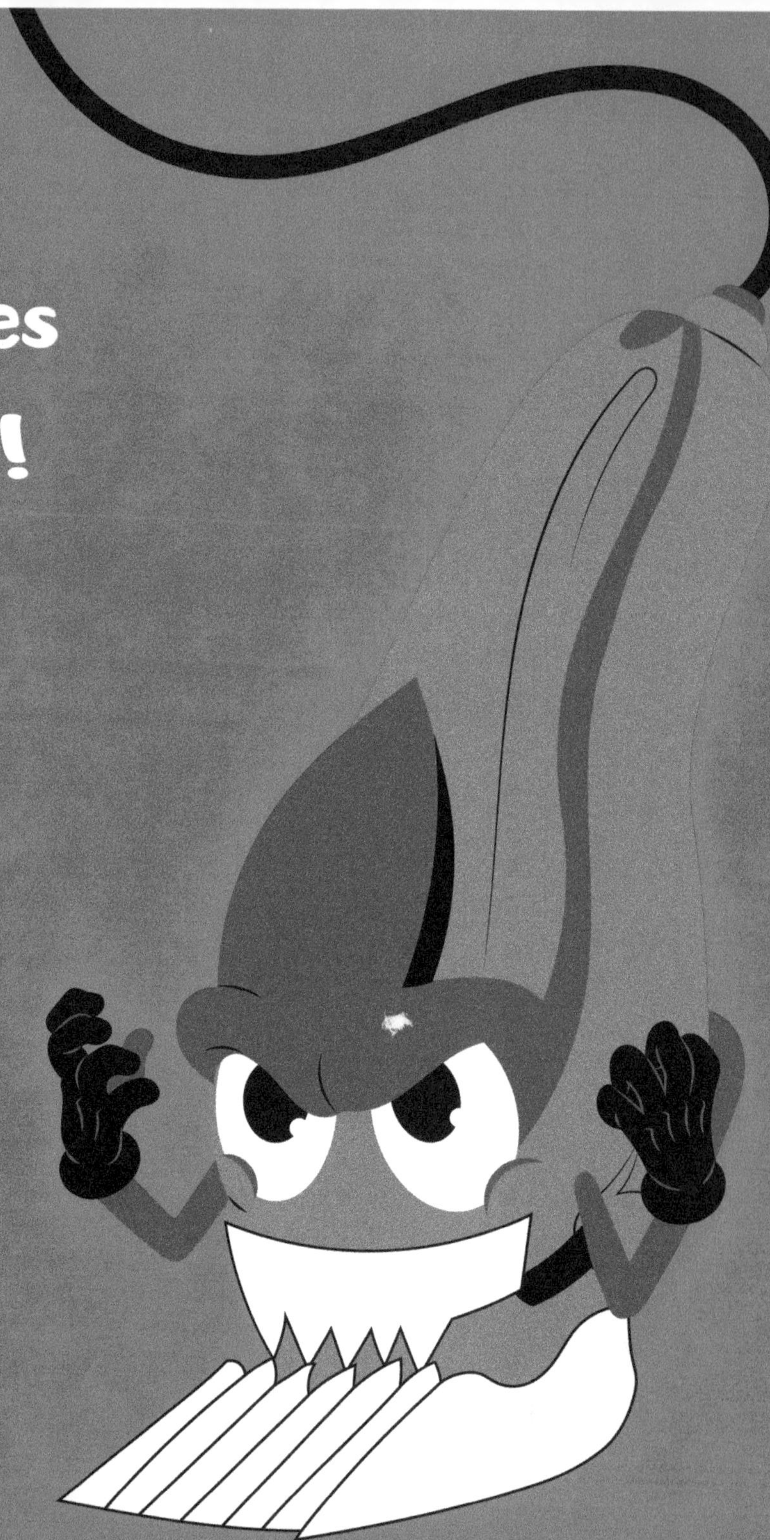

One day, my dad said
it was time for
my first haircut,
and I got scared.

To make me feel better, my daddy brought me my own set of hair tools.

It's not so bad!

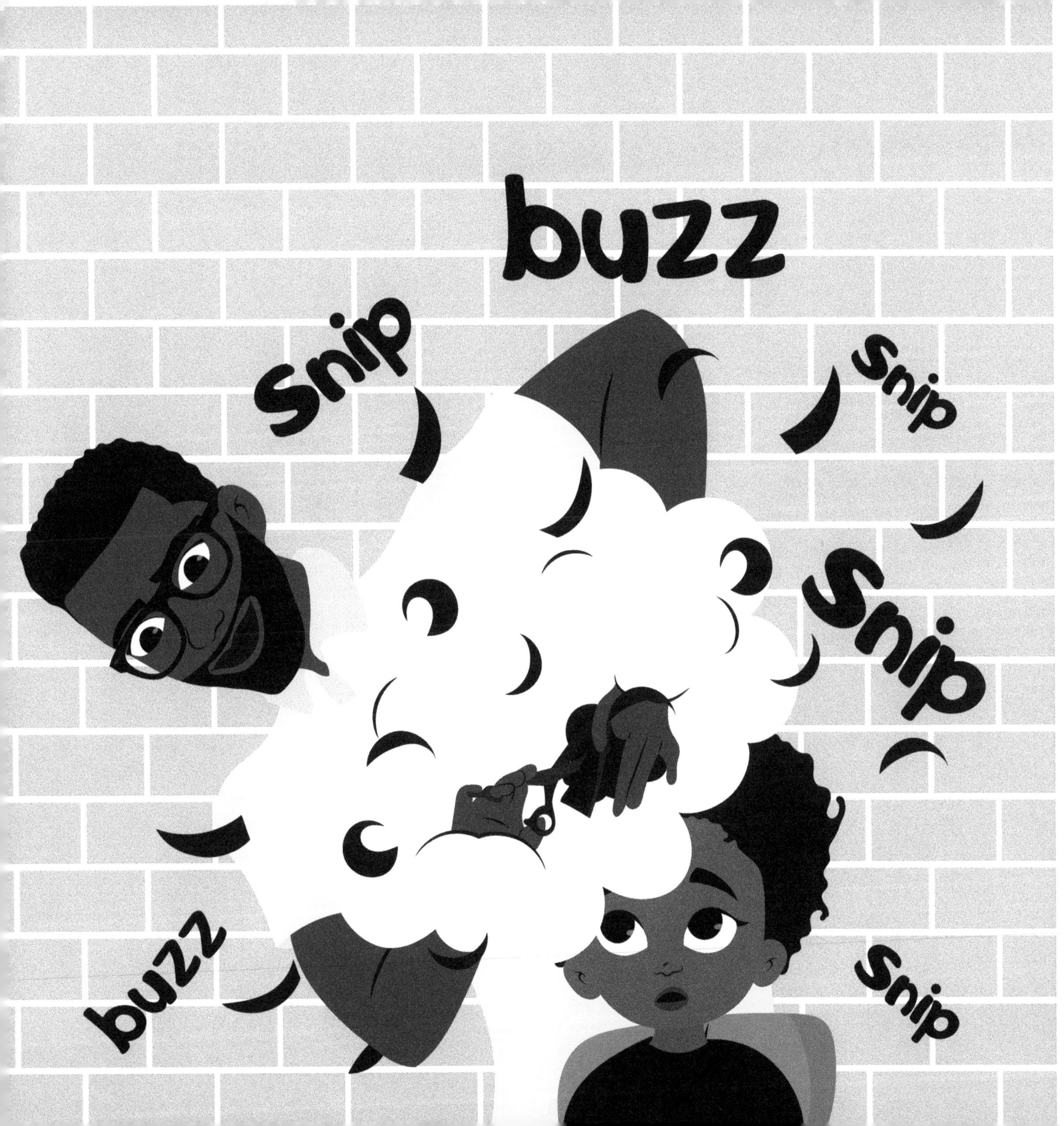
buzz
Snip
Snip
Snip
buzz
Snip

Time to see my new hair!

My new hair is amazing!

Now I love when daddy cuts my hair!

Baby's first haircut

Date: _____

Pic:

CPSIA information can be obtained
at www.ICGtesting.com
Printed in the USA
BVHW021320290721
613179BV00007B/1199